MY ONE WISH

Written by
Stephanie Ade

Illustrated by
Deborah C. Johnson

Briley & Baxter Publications | Plymouth, Massachusetts

ISBN: 978-1-954819-56-6

Book Design: Deborah C. Johnson

DEDICATION

For my own little ones who like to dream big:
Abby, Austin, and Axel!

As I held a shiny coin in my hand, my grandmother said,
"Make ONLY ONE wish, and give a good throw.
Your wish may come true. You never know!"

I closed my eyes,
thinking of what to wish.
Oh my, do I have a list!

I could wish for a giraffe,
but how long would that last?

I could wish for a fire-breathing dragon
to pull my wagon!

SUNDAY, MONDAY, TUESDAY,
WEDNESDAY, THURSDAY, FRIDAY, SATURDAY!

I could wish to eat cake every day,
but what would my mother say?

I could wish to live in a pool—oh that would be cool!

I could wish for an ice cream cone with
twenty different flavors.
Wouldn't that be something to savor?!

I could wish for a hot air balloon
to take me up to the moon!

I could wish for a dinosaur friend
named Borus.
He could be a Tyrannosaurus!

HUMPBACK

I could wish to swim with a whale
who has a really long tail!

I could wish for a boat that transforms
into a motorcycle and a car—
that would be bizarre!

I could wish to have a bed made of candy.
Wouldn't that be dandy?!

I could wish to ride a sky-high Ferris wheel.
That would be surreal!

I could wish to have one hundred puppies
to cuddle as my lovies!

I could wish to have a mountain of mac and cheese...
Maybe if I say, "pretty please?"

I could wish to jump from cloud to cloud in the sky
or perhaps that I could fly!

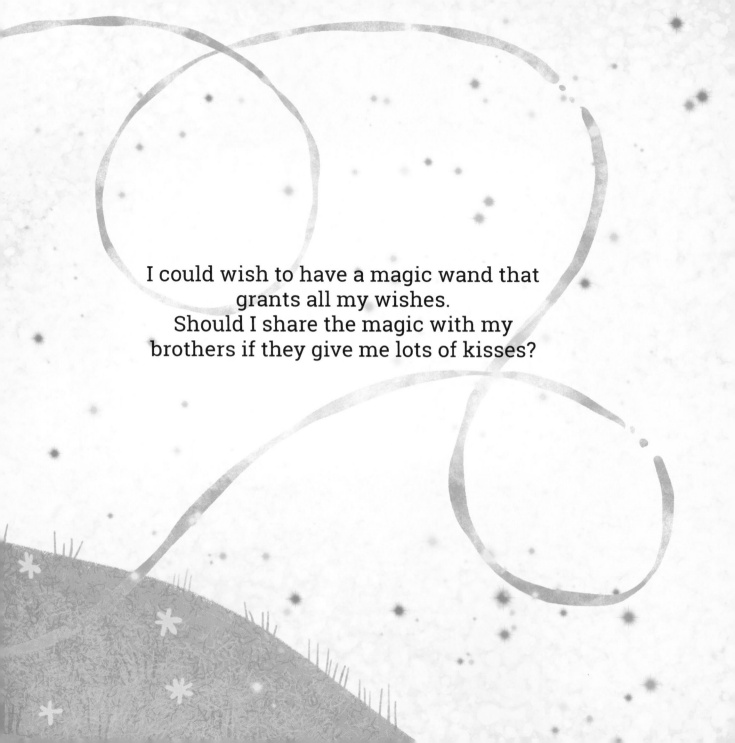

I could wish to have a magic wand that grants all my wishes.
Should I share the magic with my brothers if they give me lots of kisses?

WILL MY WISH COME TRUE?
I can't really tell you...

PLOP! After my coin splashed into the water,
my grandmother looked at me and said,
"You'll never have to wish for your grandmother's kiss!"

The End

ABOUT THE AUTHOR

Stephanie Ade was born in Boston, Massachusetts and grew up in the surrounding area. She attended Kimball Union Academy in New Hampshire and went on to earn her undergraduate degree at Washington College in Maryland. While covering the East Coast, she always had the support and love of her family to help her achieve her goals. Therefore, when the opportunity came to move to New York City to attend Bank Street College of Education, she was excited to learn how to aid children in achieving their goals.

As a teacher, Stephanie witnessed the imagination of her young students on a daily basis, so she was inspired to write her own children's book to bring these creative ideas to life. Stephanie currently resides in New Jersey with her husband and three kids, who encouraged and supported her throughout the creation of My One Wish. As a family, they enjoy summers at the beach and winters on the slopes, embracing all that life has to offer.

CPSIA information can be obtained
at www.ICGtesting.com
Printed in the USA
LVHW070636151222
735218LV00009B/333

9 781954 819566